THE LOST LITTLE BOY
Starring Josiah Lee

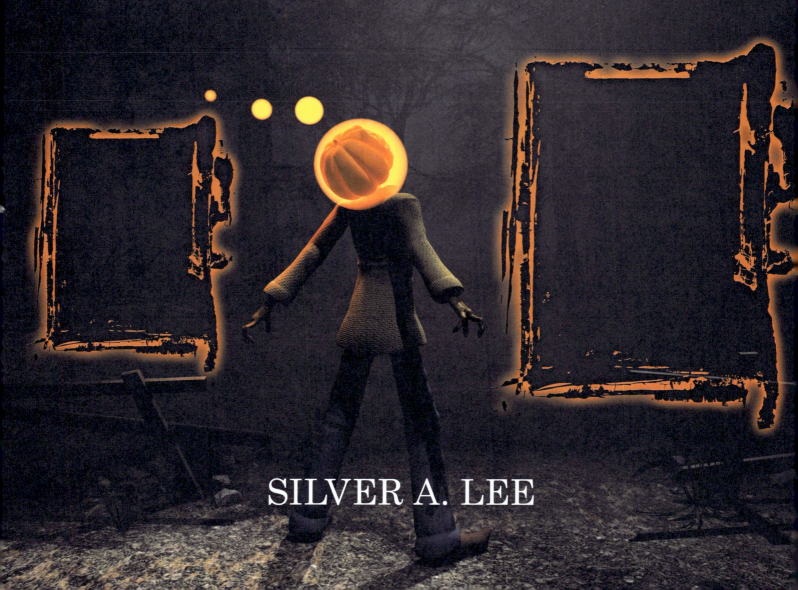

SILVER A. LEE

Balboa Press books may be ordered through booksellers or by contacting:

Balboa Press
A Division of Hay House
1663 Liberty Drive
Bloomington, IN 47403
www.balboapress.com
1 (877) 407-4847

This is a work of fiction. All of the characters, names, incidents, organizations, and dialogue in this novel are either the products of the author's imagination or are used fictitiously.

ISBN: 978-1-5043-9061-3 (sc)
ISBN: 978-1-5043-9062-0 (e)

Print information available on the last page.

Balboa Press rev. date: 01/08/2019

BALBOA
PRESS
A DIVISION OF HAY HOUSE

Contents

Series One

The Lost Little Boy

On a rainy day late in January, I finally revived my report card; while attending school in the last grade at Silver Lee School Of English. I thought to myself "I can't wait until I start the next grade." What's so weird about my school it goes all the way to eighth grade. I forgot to brush my teeth again, sometimes I just don't want too. I take a shower, get dressed, and ready for school, always on time; that's good enough for me. Besides that, I do my homework, read twenty minutes a day, I'm good. My mom and, Dad was getting on my last nerve yapping at me about what to wear and, they don't like what I choose, it is enough that I cannot get the games that I want. Then when I go outside to play, I always have to come home because, my mother thinks that some maniac is going to kidnap me.

I was like "Mom get real nobody is going to kidnap me".

Then, she continues to clean up the house before Dad gets home and, I sneak right back out down the street to my friend's house to play XBOX 360 elite.

"John can you wait until recess to talk? This is a very important subject," said Ms. States.

"Yes, Ms. States this is the easiest subject," said John.

"We only have about twenty minutes left before the bell rings, later this afternoon it is supposed to be foggy weather; speaking of foggy weather let's talk about Geography," said Ms. States, "pop question."

"Hey ask John he knows, last time he got a hundred percent," said Tyler.

"Where does lightening come from?" asked Ms. States.

"Ms. States how are we going to go out to recess, when the bell for going home is going to ring in like eight minutes?" asked John.

"Well, if you answer the question we can go outside," said Ms. States.

"The clouds said May".

"No, that's not the answer," said Ms. States.

"The sky," said Tyler.

"No," said Ms. States.

"The ground," said John.

"Very good you are correct, lightening comes from the ground, and we will continue this subject; remember children the operator will be calling your parents to notify you if you are to attend school tomorrow we are supposed to be having foggy weather. If your parents have any questions call Mrs. America, or Mr. Idaho. Okay you are all dismissed."

"What's wrong? You seem bummed out," said Tyler.

"Nothing, I did not get to answer the whole question, and it is freezing out here, I wonder what's for dinner today?" said John.

"Come on John I know you better than that, maybe you should clean your room, and brush your teeth everyday like your folks ask you too. Dude how difficult can that be?" says Tyler. "You are like the most spoiled kid in Mountain Ville never hardly obey your parents, and still get whatever you want."

"It's not like you are going to die if you brush your teeth every day," said Tyler.

"Very funny, guess what? My father said that he made something really special for me, but I think that he is going to change his mind because, I was being so called out of line with my mother the other day. I wasn't, besides I don't think he is even finished with the project yet. My dad also said that I am going to love it. We live in the mountains all the way up where our backyard is the woods. It practically looks like a forest. I was thinking maybe we can go up there in the Summer time because, it is kind of scary in the winter. It's always raining, windy, thunder, and lightening," said John.

"Heyyy, maybe it's a playhouse where we can hang out," said Tyler.

"I don't know yet," said John.

"Well, as soon as you find out go to the middle of the woods take a look around check it out, don't stay for a long time because, you have to come back to get me, and then we will go back together hiking or riding our bikes, or your go cart having extreme fun for the winter break. Au au au, and sneak some beer. Yeeahhhh!" yelling out loud with excitement, said Tyler, and John. "For reals, what? And lose our way home no way," said John.

"Well, this is where I have to turn dude," said John.

"Dude, I am going to call you I have a box full of stuff we can put into your playhouse," said Tyler.

"Okay, cool but, I have to do my homework so call me around 6:00," said John.

"Righteous," said Tyler.

And they both went separate ways walking home.

"Mom, Dad I am home! Ms. States said that the operator will be calling today to let us know if school will be open tomorrow, they don't know if the fog."

"John sweetheart I am right here, you do not have to yell," said Evelyn, John's Mother. "I am doing laundry sweet pea so put the ringer on loud for me."

"I will be in my room if you need me mom."

"Homework first no radio or video games," said Evelyn.

"I know mom," said John.

And instead of starting his homework John put on his radio, and started to play video games.

"Dinner will be ready soon please get your clothes out of the dryer and fold them up, I want you to take five pair of pants, and five tee shirts for school next week, so that I can iron them and put your clothes in your dresser. Or must I do them again?" said Evelyn.

"Mom can you make me a snack? Please." asked John.

"Yes, of course but, you have to put your clothes away," said Evelyn.

"Where's dad?" asked John, "Will he be home soon?"

"Yes, he will be home soon," says Evelyn.

"Well, in the meantime may I play my video game?" said John. "Mom, you know what? My friend he is really starting to get on my nerves," said John.

"Why, what happen?" said Evelyn.

"Well, I mentioned my play house that dad built for me, and it seems like each time I tell him about my new things he expect me to share my things. Like you better share or else. I be thinking or else what? You'll stop being my friend? What do you think I should tell him?"

"First of all you should not be telling people about your new toys there's people out there who are under privileged and may become envious of you. And if you do not want to share your things then do not tell others about your toys. But, if you do brag then on days you want company invite your friends, and when you do not want company then say you are busy, sick or something."

"Oh, I have a good idea," said Evelyn.

"What?" said John.

"Stop bragging, and when Tyler ask, did your dad get you anything new? Just tell him my folks are contemplating on sending me away", said Evelyn.

"Good idea... Mom? Are you and Dad really going to send me away?" asked John.

"Well, no but, I am concern about your behavior. Yelling out loud not wanting to obey and do your chores around the house. It is not that hard John sweet pea, it's just getting really frustrating for me and your father, we are just running out of ideas on how to discipline you."

"So instead of sending you away we decided to build you a play house in the woods. You know something special, and hopefully you will understand how much we love you. And that we hope that you come to a better understanding that while you grow you need to listen to what we tell you. It will make everything so much easier coming home from work, and not having to listen to you being disobedient. Your father gets enough of that at work," said Evelyn.

"How do you know?" asked John.

"Your father tells me everything," said Evelyn.

"So will I ever be grounded from my play house?" asked John.

"No, only because, you keep very good grades, and you go to school every day," said Evelyn.

"Oh, here comes dad," said John.

"Don't take it to the head just consider not talking back so much and being more obedient less talking back more listening. We had to make sure that the play house was walking distance, it's kind of far but, yet it is close. At times you will be grounded off of your Go Cart," said Evelyn.

The door opened, and it is John's dad.

"Evelyn! John, John, Evelyn!" He said with excitement, "How is my 4.0 GPA grad?"

"I'm fine dad, oh, dad mom said that I had to ask you could I play my video games?" said John.

"I guess you can after dinner, have you clean your room? Under the bed? Fold your clothes? Finished your homework? All that good stuff," said Dad.

"Give me a break, I can only handle so much every day I am always nonstop cleaning! You make me feel like I am a slave dang." said John with a loud voice.

"Okay, well you can start later cleaning, and do not say that word in this house," said Evelyn.

"What? Slave, oh who cares see their you go, I wanted to talk to you about something but, never mind; you would probably say No, skating, or eating out with a girl."

"I am about to set the table for supper, remember what we talked about John," said Evelyn.

"Your saying to give you a break?, said John. Well, try being easy on your mom for once. Evelyn walked into the kitchen with her head down. " Mom I'm sorry, said John". It's okay just go fold your clothes like I asked you too, said Evelyn. "Well, sweet pea it is getting late I will help you fold your clothes, and we can talk at the same time, said John's Dad." " No, I can do it, said John". I know you can it will just take you a little bit longer, laughing said, John's Dad.

"By the time we finish dinner will be ready, said Dad". While folding clothes he talked with his son about the play house but, his father did not tell him about the secrets of the play house. "You act way more excited than me dad, said John". " The reason why I am so excited is because when I was a boy I always wanted a play house but, my parents could not afford one so they'd say, said Dad. The walk is really nice not to far not to close, you'll love it.

"Are we going tonight? Asked John". Maybe, maybe, said his father. " can one of you get the phone please? I am setting the table, and dinner is ready said Evelyn". I will answer the phone said John. " Hello"

"Good evening, this is the school operator calling to let you know that school will be in session tomorrow, " Dad! It's the operator, said John.

"Hi what's going on? Said Dad".

"Most likely the weather will not start until early morning, so school will be in session. Make sure you have your seat belts on, and your fog beam lights, thank you and have a wonderful evening", said the operator.

Soon after John's father was off the phone he had decided to take his son to the play house in the woods for the first time.

"Great my favorite, Halibut, mashed potatoes, and mixed vegetables, John I made the decision to take you to the play house after dinner", said Dad.

Really, yes said John.

"We have to get our coat's, and flash lights, said Dad"

"Are you sure that you want to go to the play house tonight? It looks like it is getting kind of dark outside, said Evelyn.

"I already made up my mind, and I know that John is excited, and I feel that I should show him the nice Play house I guess if that is what you want to call it, it's more like a Pumpkin Patch but, I am not going to spoil the surprise, said Dad".

"Oh geez, your father can be a real scary man please don't tell me that you built some little weird house in the middle of the woods.", said Evelyn.

"No, it's not weird; it's just a creation something I want my son to have, something my parent's would not have ever gave me, they'd pray for weeks on end, Evelyn don't start with me", said Dad.

"I know I'm just saying because, I do believe in spooks, you should have said something I would have given you some garlic, said Evelyn. And, they all started to laugh.

I am almost finished can we go now dad? Please, please, please; said John

"I guess we can head on out before it get's late right honey? Said Dad".

"Yes, of course I will wait here in case I need to drive out to get you guys, said Evelyn."

"okay, we will be back later tonight, said Dad"

"Be safe and, here I packed some extra batteries for the flash lights you never know sometimes flash lights hate giving light – with a laugh-, said Evelyn".

"Thank you mom, said John" as he waved, and his other hand in his pocket.

"Thank goodness the fog did not settle in I would have been upset, said Dad".

I know thank goodness the fog did not settle in, or this evening, said John.

"Evening... I just said that said Dad".

John, and his father walked on a path that led from the house all the way to

the play house, not realizing that the evening before he'd forgot to finish the path way, being so tire from working but, he is not going to realize it until it is to late. Actually he totally forgot. With several minutes walking down the path into the woods, water appeared slowly on both sides without notice their became to be a swamp with trees, and sparkles of dazzle of rain. Herring the crickets, and the frogs, owls.

"okay this is the only part that sucks but the rest of the way is clear, said Dad". Well how come you did not clean it up Dad? Asked John.

"I know I had to work, said Dad".

When it get's sunny I can help, that's the least I can do right? Said John.

"If you'd like to help you can, we should almost be there let's just hope that the weather does not decide to change; because, if it does we won't be able to get through the fog son. So stay close to the path so that we will not get lost.

The sun began to set, and most of the path way was like a swamp because, of the rain.

"Almost there I can not see a thing from where I am standing oh no!" said Dad."

While john and his Dad was walking to the play house sadly the clouds drop causing fog, and the foggy weather had settled in without them even noticing. It rain so hard, and so much the rest of the path became, like mud. Looking at his watch he noticed it had only been 32 minutes, moving the branches out from the path way, from kicking the sticks, and stretching there legs over the fallen trees. Turning a slight corner with pebbles and rocks bouncing into there shoe John, and his Dad began to sing a song.

"Like father like son I am smart as you, and you are as smart as me; watch me tie my shoe, there is nothing we can not do. Hey!skip hi two, and Lu grab a pear of the tree, and take off the leaf.. And, skip while we eat."

Laughing, and laughing John loved the time that he was spending with his father especially going out to a Play House that his father had made for him.

"You wanted to talk to me about something?, with your mother, and I, you said something about a girl that you liked right? Said Dad".

Yes, why? What about it? Said John.

"I was just wondering I do not remember myself ever telling you about how relationships are, and what it's all about. But, you have you whole life ahead of you, and I just feel that you are still to young. If you really do like that girl then you should be her best friend most of her life then when she's older she will love you most". Said Dad.

Is that how you were with mom? Asked John.

"Um.. sort of but, I felt that she needed me sooner I guess because, I knew within myself that I really truly do love your mother". Said Dad.

I was thinking maybe I should take your word on it, I really do like her, said John.

"I understand but, you must finish high school, and get a nice job, said John's father".

Look a Bull Frog, John said with an excited voice.

"Yes, I see does it look like it is getting foggier or is it just me? Oh, no this isn't good here hang on to my hand John so that we won't get lost, said Dad".

But, sadly, John has strayed off, and was lost.

Dad, I'm over here! Can you see me? Said John

"No, said Dad".

And, he was walking further and further away, and soon john,and his dad was lost in the woods.

Daddy! Daddy! Can you here me? Said John.

There was no reply, only the sounds of the frogs, grass hoppers, and the whistle of the winds. As an Owl hoots from a tree John is so frighten that he trips over a branch; little did he know he had finally reached his Play House his father had built for him, trying to keep his balance he fell onto a rock, and John had passed out because, he hit his head when he had fallen. Still wandering in the woods John's dad has not found the Play House because, of the Foggy weather. Within his worried voice he yells out.

"John! Johnnnn! Oh, no my son is lost, and it is all my fault. How could I ever forgive myself? Said Dad ". While back walking home.

Back at the Play House John had finally woke up, and as he looked at his fingers he realized that he only had three fingers on each hand.

What the? With a questioned expression, aw man my head feels so heavy,

what the? What is happening to me? My head I'm a..

feeling his head, and body; I'm a Pumpkin!!!

Crying hysterically.

Oh my God! Mommy, daddy!, and all he could remember is what his mother told him. " only if you'd just listen we don't know what is to become of you and your rude behavior", so in turn he sat there, and notice that he was in a Pumpkin Patch, and the Pumpkins started to light up. While he stood there John walked around, and took a look at his playhouse asking himself is this how it is going to be all the time I come up here?

There is nothing to do, my head is a Jack o'Lantern, know one is here with me, and oh, well, I asked for it I was never nice to my mom or my dad, and now look what happen to me. What in the world is that? John asked himself.

There was a little light that appeared something like a f airy light that would lead John all the way through, and there in a mist of a shadow stood a little dwarf waving his hand saying " follow me!"

What? Now elves are coming out of nowhere? Said John.

"Hey down here, you are the young boy who has been sent away for punishment?

You was sent away to learn a very valuable lesson. I'm Zeezee the dwarf, and I am going to be with you hopefully while you are here. Said Zeezee"

Here? Where is here? Asked John.

"Pumpkin world where only you can get out to get home but, you must be very repentant because, of the way you treated your parents, said Zeezee".

Okay, so am I going to be a pumpkin forever? I understand that I have to be sorry for me being mean but, is that going to change me back? Will I be normal again? Asked John. " Right as long as you promise to be good, said Zeezee".

So, when are we going to get start going to the Pumpkin Patch, how did all of this Escalate? To me ending up here Said John.

"Well, it seems like it started at home for the second month you did not want to obey your mother by keeping up your hygiene, have you brushed your teeth? Before you went to school this morning? Or before you was led here to Pumpkin world? Sadi Zeezee.".

Well, no but, I was going to as soon as my father, and I got back home.

"But does it always take a gift from your Mother, and Father to listen to what they tell you to do? Does it always have to take gift for you to be a good son? Said Zeezee the dwarf".

But, I am a good son! Yelled John my father tells me that I am everyday, how much he loves me. " Yes, he does, and without a doubt you are I'm not saying that you are not, said Zeezee".

So what are you trying to say? Asked John.

"To respect your parents wishes, and to never disobey again"

As John and Zeezee the dwarf began to walk down a lighted path, darkness began to slightly grow covering their feet; and the Pumpkins in the pumpkin patch began to glow, and there faces began to make faces. And, as the darkness grew within the night. Clouds filled the night bright sky forming the shapes of Jack O' Lanterns giggling with laughter.

Now, Zeezee the dwarf is an elf like creature that guides who ever is sent to Pumpkin Patch. He carries a little pouch strap on his shoulder kind of hairy looking, and is very creepy orange color and loves fresh meat.

"The other kids that came here not to long ago, he never went back home. Oh, how nasty and, mean he was to his parents he cared for know one but, himself I was more than happy to send him to pumpkin world, said Zeezee".

You sent him?, will I end up there? Said John.

"If you want to go back to your normal way of living you must learn to obey your mother, and father, you must do everything in your power to make them see that you love them dearly, said Zeezee the dwarf."

Really? And how do I be mean to my parents? I am not even a teenager, and I am already on trial because, of something or some attitude I supposedly have, and I'm just being myself. I did not mean to be mean if I was... It's just that I have so much stuff on my mind, said John.

"Your only eleven years old what can possible be on your mind? Said Zeezee".

Well, a lot of things like keeping my grades up, girls that I like, and when will I change back to my old self again this head is really heavy .

"You will be here for a couple days when you are released from here you will slowly change back to you as you walk back into the mist of the woods."said Zeezee.

Wow.. I never knew out of all these years I've lived here that there is a cave, is this where I will be sleeping? " Yes, said Zeezee". Oh, I thought it was some type of spell casting, said John. " No, no spells only potions, and stones of all colors, said Zeezee".

Will I be able to find this pumpkin cave when I turn back to normal? Am I allowed to walk around and play? Asked John.

"Beware of the night creepy crawlers, and illusions of your worst fears dwell through the night. You do not have to do your apologies tonight, said Zeezee".

Well, I just wanted to get them over with, if that's okay with you? Said John.

"you must really mean it from the heart, said Zeezee". I understand but, what if the reason why I am so mean, and misbehaving is because, my parent was mean to me?, and they are at sometimes discouraging, said John.

"When you enter the fence there is a fire pit on the ground, the spirits will know if you really care or not, someone has to be the bigger person, said Zeezee, and I here that you have outstanding grades, and I think you are smart enough to listen, and clean up your room, fold your clothes; I'm pretty sure that you can wait for the video games, and to wait to play your Radio.

What makes you want to give your parents a hard time? To where they led you to this pumpkin patch? Said Zeezee.

Well, like I said before must we go through this again? Please Zeezee I don't know why I don't brush my teeth, I don't know why I don't clean my room, well for my room that is what I have a mom for. Right?

"Absolutely not, as the days go by you are getting older, and you must learn those chores because, like you said "you like a girl", and someday you will out live on your own in your own home with a wife, and children, said Zeezee"

Mean while, back at John's house his mother, and father was deeply sadden because, John was lost in the woods; maybe he might be at his friend Tyler's house we can check there, said Dad. " Have you looked outside? Maybe we should call the Ranger to go look for John, said Evelyn". What actually happen, asked Evelyn.

"It started to get dark, and the fog drop without a sign, and next thing I knew we go twisted up, and lost, said Dad."

"I can't believe this, my only little boy I...I am so sorry I wish I was more careful, I should have held him by the hand" as he cried " while John's father sat he cried. " we will find him don't worry at least he is in the back yard so big. Hope is not all lost he will show up, said Evelyn.

The next morning there was know sign of john it was time to call the Forest Rangers to help find him.

"Let's call his friends the proceed", said dad.

Mean while in the Forbidden Pumpkin patch Zezee the dwarf was mixing potion, and John was looking was looking for the sacred fenced grounds he was board, and wanted to play, and even though he was enchanted as a pumpkin boy for a while he did get a little freedom.

Cricket, cricket, cricket... Rib-bit,rib-it,rib-it, Hohhot, Hohhot, Hohhot.

"That's so strange the trees are blowing in the wind, and yet I feel no breeze this must be the sacred ground, oh a lamp pole of fire. Wow! This is cool hey Tyler check this out," said John.

Suddenly a pumpkins face appeared in the clouds and mist appeared in the night gloomy sky, as the cave bats flew through the night air. But, John remembered that he did not want his friend to know were his play house was, walking he tried to find a path but, it was enchanted, and there was no way to find a way out. Wandering about, john found a river a pretty river, thinking that it could change the spell that had made him a pumpkin boy he jumped into the river, and there he saw a gold and orange color Sea Horses.

"You must be the enchanted kid, who refuses to listen to his mom, and dad. It seems like you just might have a chance to get back home because, Zeezee talked with you really good, said the Sea Horse".

So you know about what's happening? I wasn't that disobedient was I? I mean I wasn't a bad kid I was a good son, it was just that I did not want to do the same routine everyday. But, I did brush my teeth, and I did clean my room Said John; with a sorrowful voice.

I promise, I promise I will listen to my mother and father everyday, I promise

I promise I won't talk back, and blast my radio. Please, don't leave me like this please, Said John. Do you know how I can reverse the spell? What will happen if I do not make it home? John asked.

"Whelp, said the Sea Horse my name is Flute by the way, and to answer your question you just turned into the reason why you are here, which is for not brushing your teeth, blasting your radio, and not keeping your room clean, said Flute".

Well, yes but if I don't make it home said John.

"You will turn into a spoiled yes "spoiled" you will turn into a spoiled rotten pumpkin. First you lose your teeth, and then you lose your ears, and your toes and feet, said Flute".

Ohh... okay can you help me out of here? Tell me Flute, how can I break the spell? How do I reverse it? Please tell me something. I don't want to be a spoiled pumpkin boy, said John.

"Okay, I will help you under one condition that you never be mean to your mom, or dad again, said Flute the Sea horse.

You have my word, said John.

"Starting this evening you are to meet me here and, I will show you everything you need to do, it's really nothing to it sometimes I think this brakes the time of being enchanted but, you must tell know one of this, said Flute."

So, later on today I am to meet you right here?, asked John.

"Yes, said Flute"

Ok, said John.

After that, John went to the fenced fire lamp, and saw two doors that appeared in the air it was blank it said nothing but, only darkness surrounded it, and fire outlined the door. John looked up and remembered that he had to meet Flute at the river. As he turned around and ran down the path yelling Flute! Flute! It was almost nearly dark. " where are you going in such a hurry? Said Zezee. Oh hi zeezee I am going to the river, I am so thirsty I need a drink of water, and besides I am dirty. I am allowed to bathe right? Said John.

"um, I was never ask that question before but, if you want to you may, I don't see how you are going to get clean with the disobedience, and sadness you have caused your parents to feel, said Zeezee". Thank you, said John I will be back shortly.

Running down the path towards "The Sea Horse River" it came clear that he must have been going the wrong way because, John felt like he was going up hill.

oh no! no.... where is the river? That is my only way home.

But, for some odd reason their was a back way that John was able to go, it appeared out of nowhere. "Are you there? A, kid can you here me? Said Flute.

I'm... I'm right here, I got all twisted up in the forest and I almost got lost, said John.

"The spirit changes as you change, said Flute; don't worry it is a good thing that you feel the way you do. That is the sixth way you can reverse the spell."

So there is more than six rules, or ways, or whatever that I must do in order to leave this place? Said John.

Now, in " The Sea Horse River" where Flute the Seahorse live is creepy but, also beautiful many stones was visible, normally it would be rocks at the bottom of the river but, there was none in sight. The water flowed a clear blue color, and stones giving off it's shine from the bottom of the water. And, still there was darkness all around. There was darkness in the night sky, on this second night of horror John did not want to stay but, he had no choice because, of his disobedience. Flute the Seahorse was bigger than a normal size, he look just like a seahorse only that he was really big, and colorful. His tail was orange, and most of his body was black, blue, and purple. Almost like Halloween colors. Even though he looked scary he is the nicest sea creature you could ever see .

Flute made me believe that I could get away from the enchanted forest.

"No mater what, do not forget any of these directions one, you must run, run as fast as your legs can carry you, and there you will see two doors, said Flute.

Yes, yes I remember them they are really high up, said John.

"You have to jump into the door, you can not hop into it you must run and jump okay then when you are inside you must say these words.

"River water calm as the sea change me back into a boy without seeds".

Okay, will that really work, said John.

"of course, then after that walk your way through the path and you should be back home, said Flute"

That sounds so easy, said John

"It is it, is said Flute the sea horse". Then I better get going before Zeezee comes around and try to eat me said John.

"Good idea, said Flute the sea horse."

Thank you for everything said John.

And, he ran, and ran with all his might, and the doors was slowly appeared the closer he got. Aahhhhh! John jumped into the air entering into a door and he said the magical words that Flute the sea horse told him to say. " River water calm as the sea change me back into a boy without seeds". John fell into a dark hole falling, an falling. And, John landed into his back yard, Oh my God... I'm back home, I'm back home! Mother, father I am back, I am no longer a pumpkin.

John's mom, and Dad came out the house, and there everybody was worried and sad because, of John's disappearance.

'John! Oh thank goodness you are alright said Evelyn"

"where did you go son? We was worried sick we searched everywhere for you, said his Dad".

Mom, I am sorry for the way I acted with you my behavior I swear I will always be good, and listen all the time. Dad, I...I... didn't mean to talk back to you the times that I did. I apologize it will never happen again.

"Okay, I am just happy that you are safe, and here at home said, his Dad".

When John had seen that he was given another chance there was no way in the world he could ever forget what happen in Pumpkin World. Now ever summer, and Spring John, and his best friend Tyler go to play at John's Pumpkin Patch Playhouse.

The End

"Escape From Pumpkin World"

"Yes, I can hardly wait tomorrow is the last day of school, then it is Summer Vacation. No school for three whole months,good morning mom" said John, where is dad?.

"Good morning, your father is in the garage did you get your clothes

out for the last day of school tomorrow? So that you will not be rushing in the morning", asked John mom Evelyn.

"No, not yet but, I will I just need to ask dad something really quick" said John.

"Are you hungry?" asked Evelyn. If you are hungry she said, there are some muffins, banana's, homemade snacks, salad dip,

taco salad"

"That sounds really tasty but, after I ask dad my question, and then get my clothes out and hang them up for school tomorrow, said

John"

"okay, you do not have to rush, I was just letting you know that if you are hungry that there is food on the table, said Evelyn". With a smile.

"alright, thank you mom said John. Dad, dad I got to ask you something, said John.

While walking to the garage door, aauuu... That is really nice, it is a go cart right dad? Asked John".

"Yes, this is a pocket bike, and the other one over there is a go cart. They go pretty fast, I am building a race way pavement that leads to the Pumpkin Club house. Maybe I will let you drive when you are on your summer vacation, or when you start the 8th grade. Well, after summer vacation keep up your grades, make sure you keep your bed room clean, and do your daily chores.

Your other gifts I handed to you, said John's father; this time you will have to earn them. Did you get something to eat? You'd better hurry you know how Falonie get's".

Falonie, is John's little sister, little Falonie loves being around her big brother, and loves playing with her toys. Even though she is only six years old she feels that her older brother should not mind playing with her. But, John is not the nicest brother. Who could say No to such a beauty like Falonie? Falonie has pretty light brown eyes and,

such pretty long brown hair.

"Mom! Said, John, aren't you going to stop her from eating all the food? Stop eating all the food you greedy, demanded John".

"mommie John is being mean to me again. Said Falonie".

"you know what? I was going to let you stay up for an extra hour but, I changed my mind. You know how that makes me upset when you pick, and argue at your little sister, she is only six years old. So. since you rather pick on her just because, she wants to eat you can just go to your room and, go to sleep early; besides you have to wake up bright, and early to walk to school anyway, said Evelyn."

"Man...I... that little, said John".

"What did you say? Go to your room right now, said Evelyn".

So John got up stood their and, said " what are you looking at? You

dumb little girl". Then he walked away; while he walked up the stairs, outside a spooky mist of fog began to form all around the house outside. John did not realize that his habits of being a rotten

pumpkin boy was again taking him over. John had forgotten all about pumpkin world, and how scary it was being there all alone in an enchanted world where their was only thick fog.

"momma, say's Falonie".

"yes, Evelyn said".

"why does John hate me so much?

"He does not hate you, John is just a growing teen and, he does not know how to control his emotions. He is probably like that because,

he misses being the only child. You was just a baby then, only ate milk and stuff, said Evelyn". Falonie just stared, staying silent .

"Hello, how is my little Princess? Said Falonie's dad".

"Hi, daddy said Falonie quietly".

"what's the matter? Why the long face? Asked Dad; John went to bed early? Dad asked".

"where do you want me to start? Said Evelyn your son is starting to be his old self again but, worse".

"oh, that's not good, start from the beginning to the end, said Dad".

"John was being very mean to Falonie that is why she has the long face and, he really hurt her feelings this time. So since John could not stand eating with his little sister I sent him to his room".

"aw.. not again, said Dad John asked about the pocket Bike, and the Go Cart; I told John that he has to earn the pocket Bike, and the Go cart, said Dad. How can we make him earn it? What can we make him do to work hard for the Go cart and, the Pocket Bike?".

"I have a pretty good idea, said Evelyn".

"I am just saying, he has something we want, and we have something he want's so why not start now? He can work and earn everything we give him. He needs to learn because, he will have to sooner, or later said dad".

"Your right, said Evelyn."

"My solution, we can make him work on his attitude towards Falonie

keep the yard up for three months, spend more time with his little sister so that he can learn to love her, said dad".

"This is so pristine, said Evelyn; may we sit tomorrow and talk this over during dinner along with John, and Falonie?"

"Is this dinner? Yum so healthy said Dad".

"Really, you like it? I was hoping you'd approve having vegetable, and fruits for dinner one day out of the week, to keep up with nutrition.

Save on utilities, help the environment, said Evelyn".

"That's good I don't mind at all. Staying healthy is the key to a healthy life style, said dad I am not sleepy, or exhausted I just want to rest, and relax. Oh, anyway it's not like we get enough nutrition through the week, I am going to take a nice hot shower get into my pajamas, and lay down in my big cozy bed".

"Am I invited? Say's Evelyn, I have been cooking, and cleaning all day".

"I was just about to ask if you'd like to join me but, you have to sleep at the end of the bed, laughing. Said Dad".

Meanwhile, John was on his XBOX live playing Black Ops 2 Zombies.

"Falonie knock,knock Falonie time to go to sleep, said Mom".

"Mom, said Falonie".

"yes, sweet heart".

"when do I get to go to school? Like John, and his friends, asked Falonie".

"In few months, said Evelyn".

"what's a few months? Asked Falonie.

"After summer vacation, school will start in three months so that's like a few months, explained Evelyn".

"Are the other kids mean? Will they make fun of me like John?, said Falonie".

"No, not at all not all kids are mean like that good night, I love you".

"They are both sleep? Asked Dad".

"Yes, they are, answered Evelyn.

"okay, well good night".

The next morning.

"Hey mom! I am leaving for school, said John".

"you still have a good fifteen, or seventeen minutes, you eat? Said, Evelyn.

"Yeah, I know I am going early so that I can Hang out with my friends, said John and, yes I did eat I am taking an apple".

"Know that is much better I sure wish that you can be like this every morning next school year, by love you have a nice day said Evelyn".

While John was walking to school he felt s chill over him as an overcast of the clouds darken the blue sky. For some odd reason John felt a gut feeling that he was not alone. Thinking that he is seeing things the road appeared to be changing, changing into something that he never wanted to see again. The road leading to Pumpkin World.

"what.. oh, oh! no.. where is the school? The school? Where is the? The?

No, no, nnoo.."

John curled up and, held, and hugged himself, tight, shivering vigorously

shaking with terror.

"please no, I'll be good, I'll be good John repeated".

"what's his problem?, all the school kids was looking at John shaking their heads, and the teachers began to look at him weirdly".

"are you alright? Asked Mr. Idaho".

John looked up at the teacher with frighten eyes, close to a pale face and whispered.

"I don't want to go back there, I didn't do anything to deserve to experience that, what am I doing wrong? What can I do to make it better? Said John".

"Do you want to go home? Asked Mr. Idaho. Snap out of it John you are at school now Mr. Idaho demanded, come on let's get you to the nurse.

"no, no right there look it's zeezee, said John.

"Pumpkin world has not forgotten about you, we will see you unexpectedly soon", and then Zeezee disappeared. Just like that the school changed back to normal.

John look around, got up " what is everybody looking at? I'm fine, I'm fine now that everything is back to normal. " I didn't see anything, you alright kiddo? Asked Mr. Idaho. " yeah, yeah I am fine I'm good thanks teach, said John.

"Aye! Yo! What happen? You was straight tripping, said Tyler.

"And, I was like oh, no that ain't my boyfriend, said May. Laughing...

what do you have planned for summer vacation?"

"yeah man do you have any plans starting tomorrow? Said Tyler".

"nothing, just hanging out at my club house, and that is about it, said John I really don't want to go anywhere statistically speaking being at home is a whole lot safer".

"until some psychotic person comes through the night, and cover's a house with a termite tent while people are sleeping"...

John, may, and Tyler looked at each other and, started to laugh.

"what? Swear they do everything else said, May, why not?".

"we are not celebrities in debt we are artist laughing hysterically, John said".

"Hey, I am so glad that you are feeling better, this morning was quiet an episode said May". " dang, I don't know what came over me, it felt like I was somewhere else; I'm sorry maybe I should go home, said John".

"everybody was looking like something was wrong with them, said Tyler you notice that May?

"yeah... yeah I did want us to go with you? Walk you home? Asked May.

Lately, Tyler and May was being disobedient to their parents, ditching class. So the portal that led to Pumpkin World has been open, and it has enough room for three.

"well, I don't want to walk alone said john.

"Tyler, May aren't you suppose to be in class? Asked Mrs. Grayyawn the principle."

"Mr. Grayyawn, I mean Mrs. Grayyawn, John lives down the road from us and, Tyler and I was wondering if we may accompany him home? Said May".

"I understand what you mean I don't see why not, by the way today is the last day of school. And May if I was younger I would have found that humorous but, since I am mature you are not funny.

"sorry Mrs. Grayyawn, said May".

"have fun this summer you "may go", said Mrs. Grayyawn.

Then John, and Tyler they all started to laugh, " oh I get it.. you may go "john get some good sleep while you are on vacation, demanded Mrs. Grayyawn".

"okay, thank you Mrs. Grayyawn bye said John".

Walking away from the school all of a sudden a mist from out of nowhere

began to creep upon the grounds of the walking path, trickling with green magical enchanted lights, and then their can to be an overcast that darken the blue sky.

"Hey, John do you think we can go to your play house today? Asked May."

"yeah, let's go to your play house, said Tyler excitedly and don't be so scary it was only a flash back, besides May,and I will be with you"

"I need to change my clothes I'll walk home, and come right over to your house as soon as I change my clothes, and don't leave without me, said May. "okay, we won't said Tyler, and John.

Hum, humhum,hum,huumm..., May was singing a song to herself walking along the foggy street she felt a chill run down her back. A Silver mist shined, and gloom flashed across the street but, no cars was in sight. May! Maymime! Hahahahaha.

"what? Who's there? John, Tyler stop messing around you ain't scaring nobody, said May".

Then she ran the rest of the way home, running into the house.

"Mom, dad ! I'm home, I am just here to change my clothes then I am going to Johns house to play at his club house".

"Hey, wait a minute busy body, would you like a bit to eat? Asked May's mother".

No, thank you mom see you later bye".

She ran out running to John's house, May ran all the way there. Knock,knock.

"oh, yeah, mom, May is coming over too, I think that is her at the door, said John. " okay,okay geez I'd better answer the door.

"Hello, Mrs. Evelyn said May"

May had greeted Evelyn before she could say hello.

"Hi, May come on it, what is that an ankle bracelet? Asked Evelyn".

"oh, it's a tracker not the real house arrest one but, the kind were my parents know that I am where I said I will be."

"oh, so you use to have the real one, what did you do to get that? Said Evelyn".

"Well, ah I am not proud of what I did but, if you must know I was fighting with my parents, and they called the police on me then pressed charges said May".

"you mother and father? Asked Evelyn".

"No, only my..."

"come on May we are about to go to the play house, Mother stop being so rude, and nosey just got on summer vacation we are not trying to be depressed geez, and May never killed anybody to get that ankle thingy alright. Said, John, sorry May".

"aye take a couple of flash lights because, it get's dark, and grab some snacks too, said Evelyn".

"Okay, said John. Tyler you hold the blankets, May hold the snacks in the back pack, and I will hold the flash lights to lead the way; alrighty bye mom, and Dad we'll see you in a couple of hours ".

"Think you can get to the pumpkin path within an hour? Night falls soon,

said Dad"

"Yes, we will bye okay you guys, we are going to have a gucci time, said John".

Walking down the path way John, Tyler and, May could here the birds chirp,and singing, crickets making cricket noises. Stepping over rocks, and fallen tree logs what a peaceful walk.

"aw a puddle of water darn, it feels like as if we were walking for twenty minutes already, whined May,

No, not exactly May we have been walking only for twenty minutes, said John".

"shush up, and just walk, said Tyler".

"Yeah, we are almost their anyway, you act like you've never been at the Pumpkin Patch, said John in case you do not remember we have to walk over a small hill."

"oh, yeah said Tyler.

"okay here is the spooky part, said John.

"Dude, it's cloudy as heck, said Tyler.

"you mean foggy said May".

"I got the flash lights I can barely see anything here is the hill, I guess we have been walking for awhile said John. May!, May! May, Tyler! May".

"spooky, spooky, spooky, auki, auki, auki!"

"ah, yelled John with a frightened face, aw, you to are cruel you two are messed up.

The look on your face was a Polaroid moment, said Tyler while laughing.

"we don't want to get lost on our way" putting his hands in front of him

careful this is a small steep hill.

"Hey, I can barely see the Pumpkin Patch, said May".

"Yeah, like John was saying it is right over a small little hill, said Tyler".

Cool a small little gate, au look at this play house it's amazing, looks at the pumpkins wow! Looks like they're alive, and that Scar crow is spooky auki

looking; this is scary. How did your father come up with this pumpkin path? Asked, May".

"yeah, I know tripped out hua? Said Tyler".

"yeah, my Dad is mysteriously spooky, May? Said John".

"yeah, what's up dude. Said May.

"Aaahhhhh! Screamed John, and Tyler jumping up and down, May! May your a pumpkin! A pumpkin!"

"Greetings to all three of you who have so much in common, say's Zeezee the dwarf.

"John, Tyler you guys are pumpkins too, said May".

John bent down on his knee saying Nnoooooo!, I have been good to my parents I've kept my room clean, I brushed my teeth...I...I...I do all of my homework."

Tyler stood their in the same spot for a long time in shock of fear that he would not be human again.

"Does this happen every time you come here, to your pumpkin patch? asked Tyler".

"Last time I came up here was a few months ago, you remember, and nothing happen, said John". Then John said " May, you fought your parents?"

"well, only my mom, said May".

"what is this John, some type of hidden world that changes you into some crazy pumpkin creature all because, of mom and Dad's? Asked Tyler.

"I didn't know that pumpkin World enchants anybody, said John".

Yes, it enchants anybody, only the you know, said Zeezee.

"Zeezee, said John with a surprised look.

Know one want to here a word from your mouth you glutinous child, your friend May has done awful things to her parents you should know the penalty".

"But, I didn't, said John"

Your little sister Falonie, said Zeezee.

"oh, Falonie...

"Why are you so cruel to your baby sister asked Zeezee

you seem like you missed it here in Pumpkin World I will give you sometime alone, and as Zeezee said that in an instant John had disappeared in a realm of pumpkin heads chanting.

"we hate you, we hate you we hate you if you don't love Falonie, love falonie, love falonie.

"why am I here? Asked Tyler

you forgot already? You pushed your father that is why the both of you are here May.

"Leave me alone I do not deserve this, said May"

Then what do you deserve? For the next three months, you are going to have a great vacation, and we all know that. Zeezee, and the pumpkins started to laugh.

"No, you can't do that to us, said Tyler".

May you seen all the signs, the fog, the shinning little lights you agreed to come, said Zeezee.

"No, no we didn't we didn't know that those were signs of some portal, yelled May."

May stop arguing before we end up being here forever, said Tyler.

"Haven't you heard about this? How John came up missing for days we looked in this exact same spot nobody can see us, nobody can here us, May we are in an entirely different enchanted Pumpkin World, said Tyler; I never believed John until now he said that Pumpkin World is a magical enchanted world where stones that are in the river, and they glow it's always foggy too.

"And, while you are walking around doing nothing you'll be able to think about all the bad, and disobedient things you have done to your parents, said May".

Well, they will be the only people that you miss because, your mommy, and daddy will be the only people you will be thinking about, said Zeezee the dwarf.

"what can we do to get out of here?they're has to be something, said Tyler, and May.

"forget it let it go let's just think about how wrong it is to be disobedient, and rude to our parents, and three months will be over in know time May, said."

So, without hope of escaping from Pumpkin World May began to dwell upon the kindness, and love she started to miss from her mom, and dad. However, Tyler he did not have a good relationship with his father so he went walking unknowingly towards the river where Flute the Seahorse lived, in the river. From the look on Tyler he seem really repentant, and sorry. So, pumpkin world decided to let him go back home.

"not without May, and John said Tyler".

So he stayed in Pumpkin World, meanwhile John fell into a deep sleep dreaming, in flash backs of being mean to Falonie.

"we have searched everywhere, today will be the 80th day that May, John, and Tyler have been missing. Let out support, and our worm prayer's go out to the families in sorrow schoolmates, family, and friends are afraid for John, May, and Tyler at this time they fear the worse, said the media"

Meanwhile in pumpkin World John, May, and Tyler reunited, and before they new it they were changed back to humans again.

"oh finally, real hands, and hair; wow, I learn my lesson said May".

"so did I said, Tyler how about you John? "I miss my sweet little sister said John"

Okay, well then let's go you are all free to go, and I hope you learn to work at being better, other wise Pumpkin World will always be watching you said Zeezee the dwarf.

"That is a trip we have been in the Pumpkin patch club house all along, said May".

Hiking along the path that led to meeting the News Media,

"WHY! LOOK! I can't believe my eyes like I just caught sight of a Banana split with a cherry on top, said the News caster, it's the kids".

Oh, thank you God...

Tyler ran to his Dad...

May ran to her mother, and father...

And, John ran to his little sister, and gave her a big hug.

"I'm sorry Falonie said John".

"It's okay I new you'd come around sooner, or later said Falonie"

"Dad, said Tyler where is mom?

"she is at home worried sick, said John dad".

"Are you kids alright? Asked the media.

"yeah, we're fine".

"who kidnapped you three kids? Media ask.

"Nobody we were just enchanted, said May,Tyler, and John.

Enchanted? Well, where have you kids been, all this time?, all the people are asking.

"In Pumpkin World, said May, John, and Tyler".

Everyone started to laugh saying " Pumpkin World" Pumpkin World?

As long as the kids are okay, we are okay thank you all for your support

well, we are all happy that you are safe, and sound.

THE END

Series Three

"The Gucci Kid"

"Last summer three 8th graders went missing for three months when they reappeared walking out from the woods, saying that they dwell in a place called Pumpkin World the whole time at the play house and we just could not see them. Here at John's pumpkin play house just a half mile from there back yard. John Waltkins father Mr. John waltkins landscaped a path that lead to the pumpkin patch".

"Tell us how did it feel being a jack O' lantern?" asked

Collie, the News journalist. The only thought in your mind is your parents, how bad or disobedient "or disrespectful you've been to them, say's May". First of all do you people even believe us? Asked, Tyler. Your parents has said that all three of you have changed in your daily attitudes, listening, they do not have to even tell you to do your chores twice anymore if there is in fact a magical, enchanted, pumpkin realm to help kids be more respectful, and obedient that is great. However, many people say and feel that all of you are crazy and that you nee counseling.

But, you are not answering my question say's Tyler.

Musty Booty! Musty Booty ! Yelled John in front of the entire school and all the other teens yelled Musty Booty! Gucci Gucci! laughing. Hi John, John what's up? Gucci kid what it do? You are always so fresh John. All the school mates was saying to john. " John what do you have to say for yourself and, your friends being abducted? Asked Collie"

Nothing really, just treat people as you wish to be treated, said John. School is about to start and we still need to get to class. " we'd like a normal life right you guys?, said John". Yes, said May; yes we do said Tyler. There is always after school Come on May let's go to class Tyler come on. Bye Miss. Collie, May, John, and Tyler said while walking away. "Bye kids, talk to you later, said Collie".

"Good morning class we have a special treat for all of you today. Before you young ones go on to high school you need to know about situations that can come to you when you least expect it. Or you probably do not know what to say. We know that all of you children have busy parents and of course they tell you about not talking to strangers while walking to school, and not talking to strangers while walking home from school.

Do not get into any car with a man or a woman that you do not know. If you walk to school you walk back home from school no exceptions. Never except candy of any kind from people you do not know. Smoking is deadly for example if you smoke you would not live as long as you could have when you first never did smoke. Never have per-marital sex. You can ruin your life by being promiscuous. Meaning having sex with many people especially unprotected sex you would end up mixing your DNA with who ever the boy or girl had sex with. It is pretty gross.

Also having unprotected sex you can end up with unwanted pregnancies you know having babies, or sexually Transmitted Diseases (STD's) you will get tired, you will get ugly, you just won't be you anymore if you decide to have per-marital sex. We have a special speaker today to tell you what it is like to have a virus that is incurable which is called AIDS. HIV however, there are cures for.

If it is not to late, just a minute kids. She what? Ohh...

the person who was suppose to share with us today has passed away this morning at the Hospital. We will continue this special assemble maybe later this week everyone is dismissed. " Dang, that is so scary, said May". Oh, my God said Tyler. There are better things to do than to have a death

wish right? Say's John. " yes, like shopping for gucci clothes said May". "Yeah, like staying Gucci because, I have a rep to keep up I got to look Gucci from toe to head, and from head to toe said John".

"I just want to be fresh and clean, said Tyler". And, they all started to laugh. So like what are you doing after school? Asked Tyler. My after school agenda is like cleaning my bedroom, fold my clothes for the week, vacuum the floor, and do my homework. I ain't about to repeat the 8th grade said John so I make sure that I always have my homework done everyday. "I was thinking maybe we can go hiking, and sit at the lake said, May". I do not know if my parents will let me said John; me too said Tyler. Maybe somewhere where there is more people like the park or the movies, or the mall. " Don't you get tired of staying home doing the same thing everyday? Said, May.

Umm... I have never really thought about it that way we're always on XBOX live, and building go carts, reading, or something said John. "Hey, I think I know what that assemble was all about now said, Tyler ". What? Said May. Getting board at home and having nothing to do after doing chores can lead us into trouble explained Tyler. " How you figure?" asked John.

Well, said, Tyler after you fold your school clothes for the week, and clean your room up ; what would we normally do after words? Asked Tyler. Umm listen to music said, May. And?

Asked Tyler, do homework, say's John. I like gardening and going to the Mall to walk around said, May. I would maybe sew a pillow every now, and then sewing is like my main hobby said, May. As for me I do all of the above, I clean, help my mother cook, fold my school clothes, water the lawn, and mow the lawn, play the radio to listen to my favorite songs. But, I do not sew, and yes I be on the internet said Tyler. And yes, at times I still get board so I play my games on my XBOX. " you don't read the bible?, asked May".

"No, my mom and Dad does but, they do not make me they ask but they do not force me like your parents do," said Tyler.

Dang your lucky it feels like I am being sacrificed sometimes I wish that I could be more independent, I wish I was older, said May". Are you going to do that interview with that news reporter Collie asked John.

"Yeah, that is something we can do after homework we can ask our parents and, meet up, said May.

Cool like at the Mall aren't we going to have to sit inside? Said John.

"No not really we can ask if we can walk around at the park or at the Mall, said Tyler.

"Would they allow that said, May".

I don't know maybe, said John.

"You know what? Ever since last Summer our parents has been so close like best friends like we are, and you know something else? I am so happy that we are neighbors, now we can walk home from school together, and walk to school together. I was just thinking about when I was walking home by myself one evening I thought you guys was following me and I was so scared, because it wasn't either of you", said May.

"Hopefully we will always live here; anyways, let's find our natural hobby May you like to keep your hair nice, john you like Gucci clothes, and me I like music said Tyler". So to keep us out of trouble we can go to like the Mall, go to the music store, or to the hair store sometimes, said Tyler.

You mean beauty salon, said May. " Yeah, that's where my mom goes, said Tyler.

Hey, you want to know another funny thing I just noticed?

What, said John

"what's that said, May.

We have the same P.E. Class together said, Tyler

Your right, we're like the best friends in the whole wide world to each other, said John.

"Yes, that is true but, what is true friendship? Or companionship? Asked, May".

Friendship

Friendship, is such a trip

be loyal to me.... Be faithful to me....

True friendship, it really does exists.

Don't make fun of me, see no evil doings.

Would a friend peer pressure you to do harmful things to yourself? Would a true friend introduce you to drugs an say here sniff and smoke, this is homie love? True friendship.

Never be afraid to just say NO.

Never be afraid to tell an adult.

Never be afraid to speak up for yourself.

Never be afraid to ask for help.

Never be afraid to trust in yourself.

But, be afraid to break the LAW.

In my youth I saw so many scary things that made me want to love being a human being. Using discernment and love humanity.

It's so sad to see how cruel, and evil people can be pretending that they are good.

Friendship-- is such a trip

be loyal to me.. be loyal to me..

true friendship, really does exists

don't make fun of me be faithful to me...

I am unique and I know I really ain't got no friends but, I rather be lonely then to end up somewhere nobody wants to be six feet deep and when you set me up the jokes on you not on me because, I am the best-est friend other girls really can't see me instead they are envious because, they want to be me. My name is May and I don't play when I say I am your friend I'll be there for you forever, and always. True friendship is such a trip especially realizing that it does exists.

Gucci Kid, Tyler D, and I made it back being forgiven from talking back at the pumpkin patch. I was so scared but, I knew that my friends would never leave me there because, true friends really care.

Friendship-- is such a trip

be loyal to me... be loyal to me...

true friendship really does exists.

Don't make fun of me be faithful to me....

"You guys are my best friends I would never do anything to ruin your future. Let's think of something fun, safe and good things that we can do, said John.

"I'm with you, you guys are my best friends I would never do anything to mess up your future, said Tyler".

Me to I would never do anything to make your parents mad at you let alone bring harm, or badness to any of your futures you guys are my best friends, said May.

You know what? Said, John. I am still kind of traumatized about what happen to us this pass Summer, should we ask for a couple days from school? We would be able to do that interview with Miss. Collie, and go shopping at the Mall.

"Hey kids john, May and Tyler how are you doing today? Said Mr. Volcamoore".

We are feeling okay but, not all well we we're hoping May, john, and me if we could go home early? We are not feeling to good after our accident.

"I understand but, I can not say how you feel because I have never been in that situation before; get dressed and after P.E. Come to my office alright. said, Mr. Volcamoore.

Okay, thank you said May.

"Hello, hi Victoria how are you? This is Evelyn John's mother".

"Hi, how are you?".said Victoria.

"Good, good thank you for asking said Evelyn. Listen up I made brunch and I was hoping that you and Vincent would like to join John and I. Annie and her husband Jim, we could get more antiquated, and talk about our children".

"That sounds great we will be right over, said Victoria".

"I am so excited come right on in my husband John and, I was talking about extending patio that connects all of our houses together, said Evelyn". What do you think about that?

"who me, said Annie.

I am asking both of you said, Evelyn.

I think that would be pretty neat, how about you Victoria? Said Annie.

It is not a bad thought, I mean I rather have my child playing in the back yard instead of elsewhere.

"When would you like to start the project? Said Jim."

"perhaps in the Fall or the end of summer the weather would not be to hot it will be pristine, said John do you have a friend that owns a construction company?."

'I know somebody but, I have not heard of him in a while said John. Oh, are you talking about Rasta? Yeah, he owns that Angel Roofing company, said Vincent he is also a contractor his work is top quality".

Perfect we have the builder now all we need is the design the type of material we want to install and I think that is about it, said John.

My job I work as an architect, and I have connections to whole sale goods, products, anything we need say's Jim. if you do not mind me asking what do you do for a living? I own my own business to be specific I sell technology enough about me how is your son copping with his recent accident? Has he changed in anyway? Asked Jim. Reason why I am asking is because, my child has been so different attitude wise listening to what I say Amay is a much more pleasant child to raise".

That is how our son was when he mysteriously disappeared, said John.

"Wait a minute this has happen before? Your son disappeared? Vincent said with a surprising voice".

Yes, said Evelyn like two years ago he kept blabbing about...

it might seem silly but, Pumpkin World and a human size Sea Horse hahahahaha... Kids, say's evelyn. Has thee most funniest imaginations.

"About this patio, said Annie"

Mean while back at the school.

"I will excuse you John, May, and Tyler for one week said, Mr. Volcamoore you will be able to get some sleep hopefully some counseling to help you three cope with your accident make sure that you get your reading portion of homework from your teachers so that you will be able to keep up with the class; other than that you are free to go".

Thank you Mr. Volcamoore bye said May. " want to go to the Mall to get some new outfits for our interview with Collie? Asked Tyler"

"Finally, an outing for the only girl around here, said May". You mean an outing for us said John. And Falonie always ask to come but, she is to little that is why I never let her come.

Dang there is a lot of people I did not expect this type of crowd on a weekday, said John.

"I know hua said Tyler I'm a little hungry are you guys hungry? Let's go get something to eat".

"let's get some fries said May".

Yum, that is the best statement I've heard you say all day said Tyler.

"How may I help you? Food wise said the cashier, with a smile"

I'd like three fries a parfait, three soft drinks, and three cheese burgers with no onions, said John. What store do you want to go to first?

Yum, huumm... Hey Gucci what is up? Said Collie.

Hi, we were coming to see you today after we went shopping for a new outfit since you will be interviewing us. We want to look presentable, said May.

Yes, besides that I have a rep to keep up because, I am Gucci

"if in fact that this world you call Pumpkin world how did you get there?said Collie.

We need to first get our new clothes Miss. Collie said John.

"you guys look great are those not new clothes that you have on? Collie said".

What... oh my god, you look way to Gucci kid

dang, Amay you look beautiful said Tyler

these are my boys I love you guys, you both are so handsome said May.

Okay, so tell me if Pumpkin world is real how do you get there? Said Collie.

Well, first of all I do not know if you can be an adult secondly, the reason why we were sent there is because, we was being disobedient to our parents.

"really like not cleaning your room or what? Said Collie".

Well yes, that to said, Amay but, also not doing homework, and cleaning our bedroom, having bad attitudes stuff like that.

"an so you get sent to an enchanted world so to speak said, Collie".

As John, Tyler and May spoke more people from every direction was crowding around.

"Miss. Collie weren't we suppose to inside of like a stage or something? Asked Tyler. Many people are looking forward to more in depth we want to know everything said, Collie

oh, uhh I guess it's yeah umm said John. With a speechless expression. To answer your question pumpkin world is real it is an enchanted world for bad kids that are mean, and disobedient to there parents. It is really foggy and the whole time we are deep in the Forrest. But, nobody can here us and nobody can see us said John.

"There is a pond with a real human size sea horse that can talk, say's May".

"I did not know why I was taken there, said Tyler".

It just goes to show that in the end every young child or all children should love and obey there parents so that they can live and, have a happy life. Everybody gets a fair try in the beginning no one is an adult at birth.

there are many other kids in the world who wish that they had a mother or a father like mine. Or just wish they had a mom or Dad said, John.

"Yeah, I agree, said Tyler".

"So do I said, May".

So, if anything said John always obey your mother and father.

"even reading the Bible won't hurt the bible is like a guide" said Tyler.

"If you think about it people all over the earth is really going through the same thing from man kind beginning

Disobedience, said Amay.

The End

Series Four

"Pocket Bike Rally"

Alright you guys this is it, we are going to dust these mud munchers just to show them that Gucci kid and his friends can ride. You with us Amay?

Said John.

"My trusty dirt bike did not cost all those thousands just for the looks, I can create clouts you can count on me let's do this, where's Tylerdean? Said May.

He is at the half way mark just in case anything happens to you or me we won't lose, said John.

"So what is the deal this time?" Asked May.

You want to go to Pumpkin High School in Pumpkin World? Said John.

"what no way we have to win this race, said May".

Good thing for your trusty dirt bike, said John.

"As they both starred at each other hopping for the best".

"I am not going to an enchanted High school I have already promised to love my parents and, to not hurt them anymore" said May.

So have I....I don't understand why we keep ending up here every weekend maybe it is to remind us, or maybe we was never forgiven from the start said John.

"On your marks!"

"Zeezee" said, John with a whisper.

"Get set! Gooo!!" yelled zeezee.

"when John and, May took off a fairy appeared by there side guiding them from the booby traps by the enchanted trees, bushes, and vines that grew across the racing roads."

"we are going to need to this" say's May.

Your right, maybe our fairies can help us, said John

"Keep your eyes focused, said the fairy we are here to guide you".

Can you lead us through the race? We are not familiar with these roads, said John.

"Yes, we can said the helping fairy it gets really dark and, gloomy follow my stars as long as one of you is still behind me you should win" said, the fairy.

"A vine appeared out of nowhere and, John not seeing it rode all the way up into the clouds where dwarfs, goblins, critters, demons, ghost, and scarecrows dwell. Trying to keep him from winning or getting to the half way mark where Tyler is waiting.

Fairy, said John.

"Yes", he answered.

Go tell Amay I am in trouble and, to hurry at the half way mark so that Tyler can go until I get out of here said John.

"so the fairy flew as fast as he could go, dodging the mouths of the pumpkins and the enchanted waterfalls. He was almost there but, all of a sudden a patch of clouds came.

"Oh no, said the fairy and he waved his hands and chanted " abracadabra! In me in a bubble and he popped into a bubble that glowed so bright, and then he continued to fly through the foggy thick clouds to May that John is on the next level alone and that her and Tyler had to hurry and finish the first level together".

"Here comes the Imp's!" Yelled Peck one of you must be in trouble she, said".

You are going to have to go under through the roots short cut to get to your friend it is much faster".

"Alright, I am ready! Open the Portal! Said May".

Peck the fairy open the Redwood tree and May zoomed onto the root " vroom vroom, vroom, vroom, vroom " and the fairy used her magical powers to speed her up holding her hands out firm". Coming into focus from the gloomy fog.

"what is that?, Tyler asked his self . IMP's! He yelled. Tyler tried to ride out but for some reason he couldn't.

"Come on you guys I am about to be pumpkin soup said, Tyler" in a worried voice. " Let us go! Let us out of here! You can not do this to us! We have parents that loves us and care about us, said Tyler".

A cloud of darkness slowly appeared it came into sight, a fairy with shinny gray wings that glittered within the clouds of darkness. " I am Pishogu the ruler of all pumpkin world" he, said with a deep shrieking voice. " You are to confident that you and your puny friends will get out when you fail to realize you are already here for all of eternity".

Vroom, vroom, vroom... May came speeding out from a Redwood tree root.

"Get ready Tyler let's get out of here, yelled May". And, when she rode up the hill she was riding on one wheel, and flipped up into the air. Then Tyler kick started his Bike and skidded at full speed. For some odd reason he began to fill confused not knowing what to do.

"Boy, you have know idea how happy I am to see you, you have know idea who I just had an encounter with", said Tyler . The fairy arrived in his bright bubble, " we have little time to talk John is in trouble he has been put to the next level above, I am here to lead you both to him we will just go back the same way I came".

"who is Pishogu?" Asked Tyler.

"Oh no, Please do not mention his name!, "the faries cried with confusion" Peck and, Nifty said. He is ruler over all PUMPKIN WORLD! Oh Moon Goddess please forbid his illusions

"I don't know if it to late but, he appeared to me" said Tyler.

"That explains all of the misjudgments and illusions that we have been having said Fairy. " We need to go we need to get going, May said with a worried voice.

We must know what Pishogu said to you said Fairy.

"Well…

He said that me, May, and John are to confident and that we fail to realize that we are already trapped here for all eternity explain Tyler"

He must know something we don't see, see something Pishogu must see something we don't, said Peck.

How did you three get here? Asked Fairy.

"We were walking and, it got extremely foggy and somehow we passed out an woke up here. Explained Amay".

Did you know that Pumpkin World is not only for disobedient kids? Asked Fairy.

"No, we thought we are here because, of that said Tyler."

No, not necessarily, said Niffty most of the kids, and Teens here are not only here because of being bad but, something very tragic happen there lives.

Maybe that is John, you May, and Tylers case. Say's Peck. That is probably why Pishogu came to you, we are not quiet accurate yet. We must keep going and, win this race anyway because, it may just be our misjudgments, said Niffty.

"Let's hurry, said Peck".

"Wait said Tyler"

Their is no time to explain to you now, do you want to stay here forever? Asked Fairy.

"Of course not answered May".

"No, said Tyler".

Then we better get going. Said, NIffty.

"Crow's began to say CRAW CRAW

frogs began to say RIBBIT RIBBIT RIBBIT

while the crickets and grasshoppers CHHIRRED

The wind BLEEEWWW calmly with a whistle airing through the willow tress."

VRROOMMM, VRROOOMMMMMMMM Tyler, and May pressed on the gas to get better speed.

The sun had an overcast and when the clouds covered the Sun it changed into the Moon. T'was a Full Moon and in a distance Wolf's began to howel.

And then, the Vultures spoke weirdly that echoed through the Forrest, oh, what a high pitch it was and, scary. " YACKAAAAA, YACKAAAAAAAA! And the sound grew deeper and, deeper the futher it got YACKKKAAAAAA!.

"Sounds Asif it was calling for something"

Niffty had even a better idea of reaching John even faster by casting a spell on the Vines of the tree's moving forward like a windmill

"YEAHH! We are moving even faster say's, May"

"THAT'S WHAT I'M TALKIN ABOUT! Say's Tyler"

BOOM! Oh my God, BOOM! what was that? Said May.

We are almost at the same Level as John said, Nifty

Just keep steady, and focused we passed level two so he must be on level three, Peck said.

"Precisely, how many levels are there? Asked Tyler".

Only five said, Nifty

"Tyler you know what this means? We are almost done! said, May".

Then she accelerated and went max speed.

It must have been an illusion say's Peck

Yes, I know that noise said, Nifty.

"Thrones are growing from the vines yelled, Tyler".

"Imp's are coming fast behind us say's May".

Peck turned around and thrusted his hands out and ice came out as he chanted

"Ice is cold, cold is ice freeze the thrones on vines, freeze Pishoug time".

And all the thrones became frozen.

"We need to sleep said, May"

"Yeah, I know but, we need to catch up with John and, then when we do then we can sleep look! Said Tyler a portal; that is the portal to the level where John is".

Printed in the United States
By Bookmasters